Adventures in Dreams

is dedicated to my dear friend Audrey McDaniel
who never stopped encouraging me to publish my poems.
Sadly she passed away in 2005.

Thanks to my husband Glenn, Marlene, Steven, Ron and Vicky and the rest of my family for their help, suggestions and support. Thanks to Shannon Alton and Rachael Parkin for their illustrations and support. Thanks to Chris and Marie Weller who helped keep my love of poetry alive. Also, to Lucas LeClair who started it all by saying: "That's how I think"! Thanks also to my many young friends who gave me ideas for my book. Included in these friends are: Nathanael Lloyd, Adelle O'Reilly, Joey Andrade, Dakota and Santana Alton. Thanks to Mike and Wendy of Bowmanville Zoo for allowing me to use my picture of Sheba on the back cover.

Order this book online at www.trafford.com/07-1599 or email orders@trafford.com

Most Trafford titles are also available at major online book retailers.

© Copyright 2007 Shirley Amos, illustrations by Shannon Alton, Rachael Parkin and Shirley Amos. All rights reserved. No part of this publication may be reproduced, stored in a retrieval system, or transmitted, in any form or by any means, electronic, mechanical, photocopying, recording, or otherwise, without the written prior permission of the author.

Note for Librarians: A cataloguing record for this book is available from Library and Archives Canada at www.collectionscanada.ca/amicus/index-e.html

Printed in Victoria, BC, Canada.

ISBN: 978-1-4251-3953-7

We at Trafford believe that it is the responsibility of us all, as both individuals and corporations, to make choices that are environmentally and socially sound. You, in turn, are supporting this responsible conduct each time you purchase a Trafford book, or make use of our publishing services. To find out how you are helping, please visit www.trafford.com/responsiblepublishing.html

Our mission is to efficiently provide the world's finest, most comprehensive book publishing service, enabling every author to experience success. To find out how to publish your book, your way, and have it available worldwide, visit us online at www.trafford.com/10510

North America & international
toll-free: 1 888 232 4444 (USA & Canada)
phone: 250 383 6864 ♦ fax: 250 383 6804
email: info@trafford.com

The United Kingdom & Europe
phone: +44 (0)1865 722 113
local rate: 0845 230 9601
facsimile: +44 (0)1865 722 868
email: info.uk@trafford.com

www.trafford.com

10 9 8 7 6 5 4 3

Adventures In My Mind

Do you have an imagination? Do you like to dream in your mind?
We all have things that play inside! Let's see what we will find!
Do you ever go back in time to prehistoric days?
To visit with the dinosaurs and watch their young ones play?

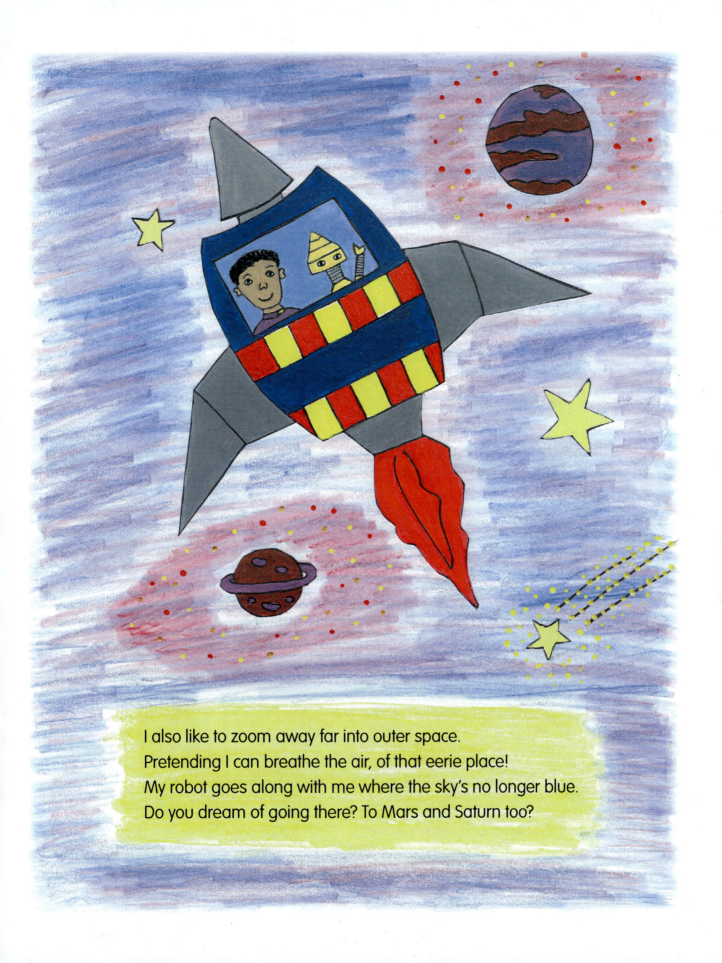

I also like to zoom away far into outer space.
Pretending I can breathe the air, of that eerie place!
My robot goes along with me where the sky's no longer blue.
Do you dream of going there? To Mars and Saturn too?

Do you ever dream of weird things, that only you can dream?
Sometimes the things I dream at night, aren't all that they may seem!
There's purple dogs and dancing cats, striped horses that can laugh!
A bird that flies up in the sky, but looks like a giraffe!

Do you ever dream that you're a superhero man?
With powers you can use for good like Hulk and Spiderman?
It's fun to have these kinds of dreams playing in your head!
I think I'll have more dreams tonight, when I go back to bed!

There's shipwrecks laying in the deep,
With treasure chests aboard!
Searching them may get you,
A very large reward!
Do you see the seahorse?
He's just passing by!
I catch the smile he gives me,
The winking of his eye!

The calmness of the water, takes on an eerie feel.
I shiver as I look around and see a frightened eel!
The fish are swimming rapidly and hiding in the dark.
I gasp as my eyes see the shape! Oh no! It is a shark!

The shark is looking right at me! I know that I am doomed!
If I don't get away today, I'm going to be consumed!
I start to race with him behind, I can't swim very fast!
I start to feel I can't go on, my strength just will not last!

Right then an octopus appears! He's huge and by my side!
I realize that I am safe, and I won't have to hide!
The battle rages on and on, the shark begins to pant!
The octopus has wrapped him up, the fish begin to chant,
"Take him down and eat him up!" "Don't let him get away!"
"As long as he is in our sea, we can't come out and play!"

The shark then realizes, there's just no hope for him!
Now his life has come to this, his face looks very grim.
I plead for him: "Please! My dear friends, give him another chance!"
Now every fish that I could see, gave me a worried glance.
The shark agrees to what I say, a lesson he did learn.
He promises: "Please let me go! I never will return!
I promise I'll swim far away, and never come back here!"
Now there's peace in our great sea, and there's no need to fear!

My Zoo Adventure

I'm fascinated by the zoo, I wished that I lived there.
A land that's filled with animals and parrots in the air!
There's things to do and things to see, of fun there is no lack.
The elephant is my best friend, he swings me to his back!
I ride just like a Tarzan pro, I feel so proud and tall!
But then the elephant so grand, trips and takes a fall!
I hit my head, it starts to spin, affecting my eyesight.
The animals are talking, asking if I am alright!

The other critters step on in, a circle to defend.
The human who had taken time, to become their friend.
The lion shakes his shaggy mane, steps closer to his prey,
The circle of the band of friends, refuse to even sway.
They once again make very clear, this human they'll defend!
The lion calmly turns and says: "Can't we just be friends?"

"No! We can't!" the camel says, the zebra then agrees.
The bashful fawn with timid voice, just whispers a small plea.
The llama too, has his say with simple and clear words.
I hear an angry chirping sound coming from the birds!
The King of all the mighty beasts, just shrugs and walks away.
Now I'm relieved that I'm alive to see another day!

My Wee Adventure

The ladybug looks down at me, she truly can't believe,
that I am standing eye to eye, she asks: "How can this be?"
I say: "It's true! Please help me, for I am lost today!
The tall grass all around me, has made me lose my way!"
She offers me a ride for free, "I'll try to take you back!"
I climb up on her tiny wings of red with dots of black.

As we buzz on through the air,
I look in sheer delight.
There's tiny creatures everywhere!
Oh, what an awesome sight!

Our flight quickly gathers speed, I see a big black hole!
It's the mouth of a hungry frog and he's on food patrol!
Ladybug has seen it too, she makes a sudden twist!
The frog is really shocked at her, when he sees that he has missed!

Now we enter my backyard, oh, look at all the bugs!
I see caterpillars, black ants and snails!
Can you see the big fat slug?

Then suddenly I hear a voice, it wakes me from my dream!
My teacher's glaring down at me! Oh how I want to scream!
I look at her, then bow my head. "I don't know what to say.
I haven't heard a word you've said. My dreams took me away!"

Monster, Monster

Monster, monster, where are you? I don't see you anywhere!
I look, look, look, here and there, I keep looking everywhere!
I sneak a peek under my bed, I find no monster there.
I look into my closet, then wonder: "Where, oh, where?"
My toy box holds so many things. Could a monster be inside?
I nod my head, that's it! It's the perfect place to hide!
But once again, there's nothing! Just toys and dolls and bears.
It seems that I can't find him...is he...anywhere?

Could my dresser be the place?
I think that it could be!
Is the monster in a drawer?
There's nothing I can see!
Monster, monster, where are you?
Are you yellow, green or blue?
I look and think. Think, think, think!
Monster, monster, are you pink?
Monster, monster, where are you?
Are you hiding in my shoe?

Are you big or are you small?
Are you short or are you tall?
Monster, monster are you here?
I don't think you're even near!
I check my bed and no one's there!
Monster are you anywhere?
I snuggle deep down in my bed.
I close my eyes and sleep instead.
I'm all alone, or so it seems!
The monster's only in my dreams!

Kitty Paws

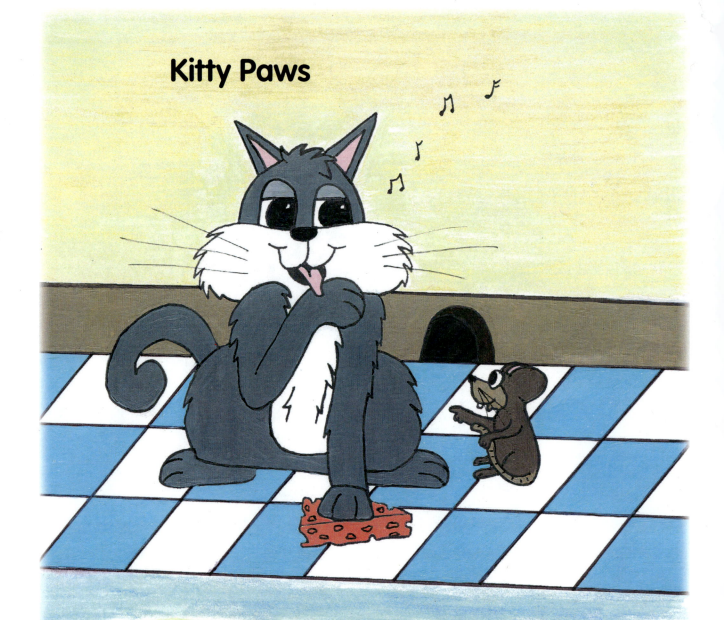

I have a little kitten. I call him Kitty Paws.
He's always busy cleaning and sharpening his claws!
Lick, lick, lick, he cleans his fur, busy all day long.
While he's busy licking, he's singing his cat song!
Sometimes I run home after school, I want to hug my cat.
But he's so busy licking, he has no time for that!
Lick, lick, lick, he's busy! Licking all day long!
Lick, lick, lick, he's licking and singing his cat song!